Walt Disney's
DONALD
and the One Bear

A TURN-ABOUT TALE

A GOLDEN BOOK, New York
Western Publishing Company, Inc.
Racine, Wisconsin 53404

Donald Duck was taking something out of the oven when his three nephews walked into the kitchen.

"Those pizzas sure look good," said Huey.

"Two of them do, anyway," added Dewey.

"What's that *other* one?" asked Louie, wrinkling his nose.

"That's my personal favorite," said Donald as he set the pizzas on the table. "Pineapple and sardines. And there's a pizza with pepperoni on it for Daisy and one with sausage for you boys."

"Yummy!" chorused the boys, reaching for their pizza.

"Don't touch!" scolded Donald. "Let me cut them. We'll go get Daisy first, and the pizzas will be just cool enough to eat when we get back."

No sooner had they left than a shaggy brown bear
came down the street. When he got to Donald's house,
he stopped. He sniffed and sniffed. Something smelled
good!

The bear lumbered up the sidewalk to the kitchen
window and looked in. When he saw the pizzas sitting
on the table, he gave a happy little growl and crawled
right through the open window.

The bear tried to pick up a piece of Daisy's pepperoni pizza, but it was too hot. He picked up a piece of
the boys' sausage pizza and took a bite, but it was too
cold. Then he tried Donald's pineapple and sardine
pizza, and it was just right. He ate one piece after
another, until it was all gone.

With his tummy full of pizza, the bear looked around for a place to rest. He wandered into the living room and sat down on the couch, where Huey, Dewey, and Louie always watched TV. The couch was too soft.

Then he tried the chair where Daisy sat when she came to visit. He didn't sit there very long. Daisy had left her knitting—with the needles in it!

At last he sat down in Donald's favorite rocker. That was just right. He rocked, and he rocked harder, and he rocked harder still, until—CRASH!—the chair suddenly tipped over backward and spilled the bear onto the floor.

Grumbling to himself, the bear lumbered upstairs.
He wanted to sleep on something that didn't move!
So first he tried Huey's bed, but it was too small.

Then he tried stretching across from Louie's bed to
Dewey's, but he sagged in the middle.

Finally he found Donald's bed, and that was just right! He snuggled down into the covers and fell fast asleep.

When Donald, Daisy, and the boys came back, Donald proudly pointed to the pizzas. But Daisy could only cry, "Somebody's been trying to eat my pizza!"

"Somebody's been eating *our* pizza!" exclaimed the boys. "Look! There's a bite out of this piece!"

"Hey!" shouted Donald. "Somebody's been eating *my* pizza—and has eaten it all up! I'm going to get to the bottom of this!" He stormed off to the living room, with Daisy and the boys following nervously.

"I can't believe there are *two* people in the world who like pineapple and sardine pizza," Dewey whispered to his brothers. Then he stopped and pointed. "Look!"

Huey and Louie were amazed. "Somebody's been sitting on our couch!" said Huey.

"And squashed the cushions!" added Louie.

"Somebody's been sitting in my chair," said Daisy, holding up a broken knitting needle.

"My rocker!" yelled Donald. "Somebody sat in my rocker and broke it to pieces!"

Daisy and the boys tried to tell Donald that his chair was just tipped over, not broken, but he was too angry to listen. He charged up the stairs two at a time. Daisy and the boys tagged along.

"Hey!" shouted Huey, pausing in the doorway of the boys' room. "Somebody's been sleeping in my bed!"

"And my bed!" added Dewey.

"Mine, too!" said Louie.

"Help!" screamed Donald from his room.

The boys ran down the hall and found Donald
hiding behind the dresser.

"Here's the culprit," Daisy told the boys, laughing.

"A bear!" said Huey.

"He's cute!" added Dewey.

"Can we keep him, Unca Donald?" asked Louie.

Donald poked his head out from behind the dresser. Seeing the boys and Daisy standing nearby and the bear still sleeping soundly, he tried to act brave. "C-Certainly n-not," he said. "We have to wake the bear and get him downstairs and out of the house right away and—"

The doorbell rang. "I'll get it!" Donald shouted, leaping out of the room.

A worried-looking little man stood on the porch. "I'm sorry to bother you," he said, "but I don't know what's happened to my Pizza—"

"We've been wondering that ourselves," Donald interrupted. "Mine got eaten all up, and—"

"No, no, no, no!" the man said frantically. "Pizza is my pet bear! You see, I own Charlie's Pizza, and our slogan is 'When you're as hungry as a bear, eat Charlie's Pizza.' Get it?"

"I get it," Donald said. "But I'd be happier if *you'd* get your *bear*. He's upstairs."

The man ran upstairs yelling, "Pizza! Pizza!"

The bear woke up when he heard the man's voice and greeted him affectionately. Charlie snapped a leash to Pizza's collar, and the bear followed him down the stairs and out the door.

"Whew!" breathed Donald. "I'm glad that's over!"

"It was kinda exciting, though," said Huey.

"Let's eat!" said Dewey.

"Yuck! Cold pizza," said Louie.

Just then the doorbell rang again. It was Charlie, holding three big boxes.

"I want to give you this reward for finding my bear," he said. "Three piping-hot, extra-large pizzas."

"Hurray!" the boys cheered.

"How very kind!" said Daisy.

"I hope you like them," Charlie added. "They're Pizza's favorite—pineapple and sardine. Thanks again for finding him!"

Huey, Dewey, Louie, and Daisy stared glumly at
the pizzas, but Donald grinned from ear to ear. "I liked
that bear from the moment I saw him," he said. "Now,
let's eat!"